1992

Robert Quackenbush

EVIL UNDER THE SEA

A Miss Mallard Mystery

Pippin Press
NEW YORK

J

Published by Pippin Press, 229 East 85th Street
Gracie Station Box 92
New York, N.Y. 10028

Printed in the United States of America
by Horowitz/Rae Book Manufacturers, Inc.

10 9 8 7 6 5 4 3 2 1

Library of Congress Cataloging-in-Publication Data

Quackenbush, Robert M.
  Evil under the sea : a Miss Mallard mystery
    p.   cm.

  Summary: Jacques Canard, noted undersea
explorer, asks Miss Mallard to help discover who is
destroying the coral in Australia's Great Barrier Reef.
[1. Mystery and detective stories.
2. Coral reefs and islands—Fiction.
3. Ducks—Fiction.]   I. Title.
PZ7.Q16Ev 1992   91-46549
[Fic]—dc20   CIP
ISBN 0-945912-16-1   AC

FOR PIET AND MARGIE,

and for

the fourth graders at Lincoln School,

Buenos Aires, Argentina,

who inspired me to tell this story

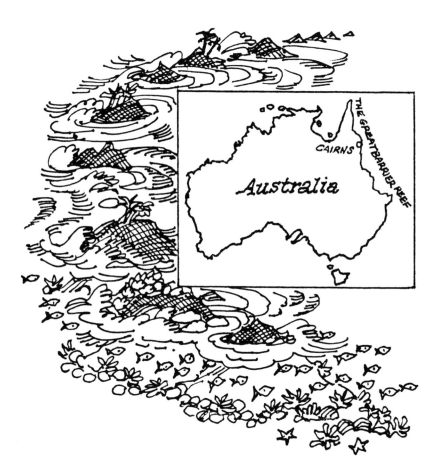

Miss Mallard, the world-famous
ducktective, leaned forward and gazed out
the airplane window. Below she saw Australia's
Great Barrier Reef gleaming in the dawn light.

"What beauty and splendor!" she said aloud.

Moments later the airplane landed at Cairns,
Queensland, on the mainland. Jacques Canard,
the noted undersea explorer, and his driver, Paul
Teal, met Miss Mallard at the airport. They all
climbed into a jeep and headed for Jacques's
boat. On the way, Jacques pointed out some of
the local sights, including his hilltop house and
Paul's beach cottage.

"It was good of you to come," said Jacques. "As
I wrote you, someone is destroying the coral on
the Great Barrier Reef. At present, the damage is
small. But the destruction could spread along
the 1250 mile Reef with its hundreds of tiny
islands. As you know, coral is the ocean's natural
filter, supplying the oxygen that fish need to
breathe. We need your help to get to the bottom of
this."

"I'll do what I can," said Miss Mallard.

Just then, Paul swerved the jeep to avoid a
truck that came racing toward them.

"KEE-RA-ZY DRIVER!" quacked Paul at the truck as it whizzed by.

"That's the second time today that has happened," said Jacques. "One would think that driver is out to get us. I know that it was the same driver because both times he was wearing a black baseball cap."

"Hmmm," said Miss Mallard.

Soon afterward they arrived at the pier where Jacques's boat was docked. While Paul was placing Miss Mallard's suitcases on board, Jacques introduced her to his crew, Dick Tree Duck, Max Merganser and Bob Gadwall.

"Dick, Max, and Bob used to share the beach house where Paul lives," said Jacques. "Now they make their home on the boat. They are never out of their scuba diving gear."

Paul climbed back on the pier.

He asked Jacques, "What else can I do?"

"Nothing now," answered Jacques. "We'll go scuba diving at the Reef to show Miss Mallard the damaged coral. I'll phone you if we need you again. In the meantime, see if you can find out who was driving the truck."

"Will do," said Paul, as he jumped into the jeep and drove off.

"So long, mate," Bob and Max called after him.

Everyone climbed aboard. Miss Mallard went below and changed into a bathing suit. Then she put on a waterproof vest with pockets to carry any clues that she might find.

When she got back on deck, Miss Mallard saw that the boat was headed for the Great Barrier Reef. She stood at the rail and admired the view. Out of the corner of her eye, she saw Bob Gadwall and Max Merganser going below. She followed them and caught them handling her knitting bag.

"We're just setting it in a better position," said Max. "It almost fell over."

"It's our job to check on things," said Bob.

Soon the boat came to a tiny island and the crew lowered the sails and dropped anchor.

"This is the place," said Jacques to Miss Mallard. "Come, and I'll show you the damage."

With that, the crew helped them into their gear and the two divers splashed off from the boat to explore the deep. Jacques led the way.

Miss Mallard was excited. She saw brightly colored brain corals, fan corals, and star corals. Tropical fish of many shapes and sizes swam among them. A world of splendor lay before her, like a garden under the sea.

Suddenly they came to a different part of the Reef. Miss Mallard was shocked by what she saw. She felt as if she were in a coral graveyard. Gone were the brilliant colors that she had seen before. Everything was chalky white. A powder as fine as new-fallen snow covered the skeletal remains of coral. Miss Mallard realized that they were now swimming along the destroyed coral that Jacques had described.

All at once, Jacques pointed at something coming their way. It was a giant shark! In a flash they hid under a low ridge. As the shark passed overhead, a tooth fell from its huge jaw. Miss Mallard caught the tooth as it floated past her.

The shark disappeared into a cave. Miss Mallard and Jacques watched and waited until they were sure it was safe to leave. Then they hurried back to the boat.

Jacques got to the boat first. He looked around and didn't see Miss Mallard. In a flash, he climbed on board. Dick Tree Duck rushed to help him out of his gear.

"Forget that!" quacked Jacques. "Find Miss Mallard! There's a shark down there!"

Just then, Miss Mallard surfaced and heard him.

"Fiddlesticks!" she said, holding up the shark's tooth. "There are no sharks in these waters. Have a look at this tooth that fell from the so-called shark that we saw. It's plastic!"

Dick pulled her onto the deck. But he did it in such an awkward way that Miss Mallard almost dropped the tooth in the water. But she caught it just in time.

"Sorry," said Dick. "It was an accident."

Jacques looked at the bit of plastic and said, "This means that the shark is mechanical and is motor-driven."

"Yes," said Miss Mallard. "I suspect that it is used for transportation and to scare divers away. The cave might be its home base. And did you notice how warm the water felt in the region where the dead coral was found?"

"You noticed it, too!" exclaimed Jacques. "Above-normal water temperature kills coral. We've got to find out what is causing the heat."

He turned to Bob Gadwall and said, "Radio the police on the mainland for help."

"But the radio isn't working," said Bob.

Jacques ran below and came back in a flash.

"The radio had a faulty tube," he said. "Fortunately I found a spare one in my tool kit and called the police. Bob, you and Miss Mallard stay on board and flag them. The rest of us will watch the entrance to the cave. We'll take a rope with us to tie up the fake shark if it comes."

Miss Mallard exclaimed, "You must take me with you! I always see a case to the finish!"

Miss Mallard got her way. She splashed from the boat with Jacques, Max, and Dick. She swam with them to the coral graveyard. But no sooner had they gotten there than the mechanical shark came bursting out of its cave and barreled toward them.

Hurriedly, they all grabbed the rope and began wrapping it around the shark. But the shark was too powerful for them. The rope broke and they were chased helter-skelter.

Miss Mallard looked for a place to hide. She headed for the entrance of the shark's cave.

"I'll conceal myself here," she thought. "Then when the shark is out of sight, I'll swim back to the boat and warn the police that we failed in our attempt to capture the shark."

Miss Mallard peered from the entrance of the cave as she waited for the right moment to escape. Suddenly everything went wrong. The shark quickly drove Jacques and the others back to the boat. Now it was heading straight for her!

There was nothing for Miss Mallard to do but to go further into the cave. She saw a light and swam toward it. The next thing she knew she was in a chamber. Before she could turn around and go back, a door slammed shut behind her. After that, water began to flow from the chamber and was soon replaced by air. When only a little of the water remained, Miss Mallard waded through it to another door. She opened it and saw an amazing sight.

There before her lay a huge city under the sea. She saw a crowd gathered before a masked figure who was speaking from a platform. She quickly got out of her diving gear and put on a worker's robe that was hanging on a nearby hook. Then she stayed in one corner and listened.

"The time has come," said the masked figure, whose voice came booming over loudspeakers. "I, Dr. Decoy, the master of our secret city, Duckopolis, will soon be the master of the world. And you, my loyal followers and workers, will help me to carry out the plan. First we will destroy the coral of the Great Barrier Reef with our lasers. Then we will send messages to world leaders that we will do the same to the other great reefs around the globe unless they do as I command. They will bow to my wishes because without coral the fish and plant life of the oceans and seas of the world will die. This would cause worldwide famine. We know it and the world leaders know it. THE KEE-RA-ZY FOOLS! CONQUER THEM WE WILL!"

With that, Dr. Decoy raised his wings and the crowd chanted, "DR. DECOY! DR. DECOY!"

"I've got to stop them," thought Miss Mallard.

She moved cautiously up a flight of stairs. She passed a control room and saw two television screens and recorders. One screen showed Dr. Decoy. The other screen showed the mechanical shark landing. Out stepped the pilot of the sharkmobile. He was wearing a black baseball cap!

"The driver of the killer truck!" thought Miss Mallard. "I must move fast!"

She raced up the stairs and flung open a door. She was surprised to see a huge room that was filled with dynamos and machinery making a lot of heat and noise.

"So this is what is killing the coral around Duckopolis!" she thought.

She climbed to a balcony above the machinery. Grabbing a monkey wrench from a worktable, she dropped it into the midst of giant turning wheels. All at once, sparks flew in all directions and the wheels came to a screeching halt. At the same time, alarm bells went off.

Everyone began running in all directions to escape hatches. Miss Mallard ran to the control room and stuffed a videotape of Dr. Decoy's talk in her waterproof vest. At the same time, she saw Dr. Decoy on one of the television screens making a solo getaway in the sharkmobile.

It soon became difficult for Miss Mallard to breathe. Then she realized that the machines that she had broken were the same ones that produced Duckopolis's air and power.

"No wonder everyone is in such a hurry to leave," she thought.

At that moment, she saw water beginning to seep in from the ceiling. Quickly, Miss Mallard raced to put on her diving gear and headed for the main entrance chamber. Soon the chamber became packed with escapees from Duckopolis. Miss Mallard edged her way to the escape door. As soon as the chamber filled with water and the escape door opened, she swam ahead of everyone else to the entrance of the cave. Then, with a mighty push of her feet, she thrust herself upward. She got away in the nick of time, as did everyone else, just as the sea reclaimed Duckopolis.

When Miss Mallard got to Jacques's boat, she saw that the police had arrived. Jacques and a police officer helped her on board.

"Meet the chief of police, Captain Pintail," said Jacques to Miss Mallard.

"Captain, quick!" said Miss Mallard. "Arrest the swimmers who are surfacing. They are all criminals. Their leader is Dr. Decoy. Under his orders, they built a secret city beneath the sea so they could make plans to take over the world. I threw a monkey wrench into their scheme. Unfortunately, Dr. Decoy escaped."

Captain Pintail went into action. He ordered the swimmers to be loaded onto the police barge and hauled off to jail. Afterward, he stayed behind to get all the facts.

"We are very grateful to you, Miss Mallard," said Captain Pintail. "But no one on the barge will tell us the identity of Dr. Decoy. If they know, they won't talk. They say he wore a mask all the time. What a crazy nut!"

"What did you just say?" said Miss Mallard, surprised. "Never mind, I heard you. Something you just said made the identity of Dr. Decoy clear to me. But I have to do one last bit of investigation before I can say for sure. We must go to the mainland."

An hour later, Jacques's boat docked at Cairns. Everyone gathered in the front yard of the beach cottage where Jacques's driver, Paul, lived.

"Why have you brought us to the place that Dick, Max, and I once shared?" asked Bob Gadwall. "Are we suspects in this case?"

"Everyone is a suspect," answered Miss Mallard.

She went to have a look at Paul's boathouse at the back of the cottage. The moment she returned, Paul came out of the cottage and stood on the porch.

"Why are all of you here?" asked Paul, puzzled.

Miss Mallard said, "Everyone, meet Dr. Decoy."

Each of the suspects looked at one another.

"I mean you, Paul," said Miss Mallard. "Drop the innocent act. I knew that you were Dr. Decoy when I remembered something that you said at Duckopolis. You said the word 'KEE-RA-ZY' the same way you said the word when you were driving the jeep. 'KEE-RA-ZY DRIVER! you yelled at the truck driver. 'KEE-RA-ZY FOOLS!' you shouted at Duckopolis, which I have on videotape in my knitting bag."

Paul quacked, "YOU'RE KEE-RA-ZY!"

"There!" said Miss Mallard. "You said it again. Besides, the one member of your gang who knows your identity has already been arrested. It will be only a matter of time before he talks."

"Who is that?" quacked Paul.

"The truck driver who tried to cause the jeep to crash," said Miss Mallard. "I know now that the near-accident was planned. It was another of your decoys to make it look as if someone was after you, Jacques, or me. You did it so no one would suspect you."

"Paul!" quacked Jacques. "So that's why you begged me to let you work for me! You wanted to spy on us to find out how much we knew about your evil scheme."

Paul started to run.

"Stay where you are," said Captain Pintail, grabbing him. "You're under arrest."

Miss Mallard said, "Captain, the mechanical shark that Dr. Decoy and his accomplice used to speed to and from Duckopolis is in Paul's boathouse behind the cottage. I discovered it a few minutes ago. That is the final proof that Paul is truly Dr. Decoy."

They all went to Paul's boathouse and there before them was the sharkmobile. With that, Paul was taken off to jail.

After Paul's arrest, Jacques said, "Thanks to you, Miss Mallard, the Reef is saved. Eventually the coral that Dr. Decoy damaged will grow back."

"That's good news," said Miss Mallard.

"The case is quacked!" said Bob Gadwall. Now let's celebrate!"

"Hurray!" said Max and Dick.

"Good idea," said Jacques. "What is your pleasure, Miss Mallard?"

"I'd love a spot of tea under some shady palms," Miss Mallard replied. "Then a swim before dark, of course."

"Of course!" said Jacques and his crew.

And off they went, quacking merrily all the way.